Deja & ME

"Deejay Saves the Day"

By

Shakia A. Johnson

Dedication

This book is dedicated to young boys of color all over as a simple expression of gratitude from the world for how much value you add to the planet just by being your beautiful brown self. Your smile makes the world a better place, and there is no limit to what you will accomplish. Reach for all of your goals. We love you, Black Boys.

Hey there! It's me, Deja the chocolate, confident conscience of young brown girls all over the world! I am so excited you're in for a treat, as I have someone special that I want you to meet. There is a bond like no other, and that's the one between a sister and a brother!

Young men, I want to introduce you to my twin brother, Deejay. He's smart and swaggy in every way! Deejay is a science and math whiz and has the perfect formula for you to enjoy; all the ingredients needed for "Black Boy Joy." Well, that's all from me. I'll let him take it away. Deejay, the boys need you to help save the day!

Hey, guys, what's up? Deejay is the name; math and science are my game! According to my calculations, everyone wants to know just how special we are, what makes us so powerful. Well, I'll let you in on a little secret.

I've solved what no man has ever been able to do! I have the perfect formula for what makes us just who we are! Put on your lab coats; grab your calculators; we're on our way! Come on, Black Boys, let's save the day! You may find words that you may not know, but not to worry, I'm here to help your vocabulary grow!

I've tested the ingredients, added and subtracted some too. To solve the equation, here is what we must do: add **RESPECT**, and times it by two!

Black Boys are respectful to everyone we encounter. We say "Yes, Ma'am" and "No, Sir" because that is what we are taught. This respect is earned; it can't be bought! We hold doors for young ladies because we're oh so swell.

We learned from our parents; they teach us so well. Respect is using our manners, saying "Please" and "Thank you." Respect is caring for others and treating them kindly. We'll times it by two because it's hard to find, but not from us; oh, no way! Being a respectful Black Boy is the only way! Be nice to everyone, no matter what they may say, for it is respect that will take us a long way. Hmm … let's see what's next in my bag. Respect ^2. Now let's add the **SWAGG.**

e·qua·tion

/əˈkwāZHən/

noun

noun: **equation**; plural noun: **equations**

1. Mathematics, a statement that the values of two mathematical expressions are equalen·coun·ter

/in'koun(t)ər,en'koun(t)ər/ *verb*

verb: **encounter**; 3rd person present: **encounters**; past tense: **encountered**;
past participle: **encountered**; gerund or present participle: **encountering**

1. unexpectedly experience or be faced with (something difficult or hostile)

in·gre·di·ent

/in'grēdēənt/

noun

noun: **ingredient**; plural noun: **ingredients**

1. a component part or element of something

Swag is what we have that makes us oh so cool. You see, swag is what makes everyone want to be like you and me! It's how we dress and how we talk. Swag is in our DNA; you can tell by how we walk! It's in our dance moves, the rhythm of our ancestors and how we groove. My oh my! We, Black Boys, sure are fly! We are admired by all when they see us walk by. Swag is the proof of confidence that we're special; it just seeps through our pores. King, no one on this planet has swag like yours! When creating this formula, I had to be sure I had the perfect code, but I think I may have gone overboard. SWAG overload! We're as sharp as a tack. Being Black Boys, there is nothing we lack; we can do and be anything as a matter of fact! Let's see here; we've got respect and swag. So far, so good, I can't complain, but we, Black Boys, are smart, so let's add the **BRAIN!**

DNA

/ˌdē ˌen ˈā/
noun

Biochemistry
noun: **DNA**; noun: **deoxyribonucleic acid**
1. deoxyribonucleic acid, a self-replicating material which is present in nearly all living organisms as the main constituent of chromosomes. It is the carrier of genetic information.
   - the fundamental and distinctive characteristics or qualities of someone or something, especially when regarded as unchangeable.

noun

noun: **ancestor**; plural noun: **ancestors**

1. a person, typically one more remote than a grandparent, from whom
   one is descended

Listen up! Class is in session. **Brains** are an important part of who we are, Black Boys! The brain is our special tool, the one that helps us to do well in school. Being smart is very cool! Using our brains can take us a long way! Look at us now! Creating "Black Boy Joy" to help save the day. Our brains help provide us with knowledge so that when we become black men, we can go to college! We will graduate with honors and become CEOs using our brains; there is no limit to where we'll go! We can use our brains to help us make good choices, to help take a stand for what's right and use our voices. Being smart is always in style, and style never fades. Black boy, let's use these brains and get good grades. The brain is what keeps us wise. If we all work together, then together we will rise! Do you have your calculator? Good! Let's put it to use: **Respect^2 + Swag+ Brains** = WAIT ... it's not quite complete! I've got one more ingredient; it's really neat. You're going to need your goggles for this one. Hold onto your seats; this one is massive; it will knock you off your feet! Respect, swag, and brains. How much more greatness could we possibly contain?!

CEO

/ˌsē ˌēˈō/

noun

noun: **CEO**; plural noun: **CEOs**

1. a chief executive officer, the highest-ranking person in a company or other institution, ultimately responsible for making managerial decisions

knowl•edge/ˈnäləj*noun*:

facts, information, and skills acquired by a person through experience or education; the theoretical or practical understanding of a subject.

This last ingredient is full of power and strength from within. The last ingredient is the <u>color</u> of our skin! That's right, Black Boy; our melanin is what makes us full of joy! Our skin tone has power as strong as kryptonite. We come in all shades, from the tan of sands to the darks of midnight; all made precious in God's sight! This formula is ours, not to be mistaken. It's who we are, and it could never be taken. You should feel proud to have helped solve this equation. The formula is just right for future generations of Black Boys like you and me just so they know all that they are and what they can be!

mel•a•nin

/'melənən/

noun

noun: **melanin**

1. a dark brown to black pigment occurring in the hair, skin, and iris of the eye in people and animals. It is responsible for tanning of skin exposed to sunlight.

kryptonite

/ˈkriptəˌnīt/

noun

noun: **kryptonite**

- something that can seriously weaken or harm a person or thing.

Just look at all the great Black Boys that have used this formula! Dr. Martin Luther King Jr. used it to help save the day. He used **Respect** to fight for freedom by saying, "I have a dream today!" He didn't have to fight or be mean. Just by using his voice, he reigned supreme, making it possible for Black Boys like you and me to have a chance at equality. Now we stand on his shoulders for the world to see just how special it is to look like us! Oh what joy it is being a Black Boy!

Superstar ball player Lebron James used his **BRAINS** and built a school for another Black Boy's gain so they, too, can learn and chase after all the dreams that their hearts yearn. See? Told you from the start it pays to use your brains, Black Boys. We are VERY smart! Wow! What an inspiration to us all!

And we all know 44th President Barack Obama was the swaggiest of them all! He used his **SWAG** to lead America in a way that only Black Boy Joy could do. Our first black president. If he can do it, so can you!

Black Boy Joy is a special bond in which we share with little Black Boys everywhere! You now have the ingredients, formula, and equations down to help spread Black Boy Joy all around town! Be proud of who you are, Black Boy. Self-love is the best lover. Never lose sight; this formula will help you take your love for self to a new height! Stay true to who you are, Black Boy. Don't change a thing. Just by being you, look at all the joy you bring! I've given you the formula and shown you what you can accomplish, but do you believe it? Will you use your Respect, Swag, and Brains to achieve it? I know the power you hold, and Black Boy Joy has power! Everyone may not understand it, and that's OK. Let nothing hold you back; let your joy shine on anyway! Maybe not now, but soon they will see your melanin is magic! Now that you know what we are made of, don't keep it to yourself. Bring other Black Boys to our lab so they, too, can learn about the value of their wealth! We're all done now; let's clean up our mess and put everything away! Grab your calculator and goggles and go use your Black Boy Joy to save the day!

About the Author

Shakia A. Johnson, a native of Baltimore, MD, is a self-starting go-getter. She proudly attended the first historically accredited Black Institution of higher learning, The Lincoln University of PA. She now continues her studies, attending University of Maryland, Baltimore County. Her entrepreneur spirit and business-orientated mindset has led her to start many different avenues of organizations. After cheering for 15 years, in 2014, Shakia turned her love for cheerleading into a coaching career when she founded Poison all-star cheerleading LLC, a traveling competition team teaching students ages 5–18. She is also the head cheerleading coach for an all-girls high school in the heart of Baltimore. After becoming a coach to so many young women, she then realized that her purpose was much greater and that it was her duty to be able to reach and touch so many more young lives. She is now a therapeutic mentor with the Catholic Charities of Baltimore. Along with servicing the next generation, Shakia thrives off the success of likeminded women. In 2018, she founded S.H.E. (sisters helping and empowering) Youth mentoring and Coaching services where she utilizes her talents for teaching and coaching to help assist other coaches and teams to build their team morale and skillset. Shakia's passion for the sport of cheer and teaching life lessons through the sport has landed her many opportunities working alongside celebrity dance coaches and traveling. Shakia continues to use all that she was given to help encourage others to step out on faith and to walk in their purpose unafraid. Now a successful businesswoman, Shakia will continue to strive toward all that she wishes to accomplish. Shakia serves as a Notary Public for the state of Maryland and is a proud member of the Naomi Grand Chapter of The Order of the Eastern Star and Delta Sigma Theta Sorority, Inc.

Feel free to stay connected with Shakia at www.CoachWithKia.com. Or by email at hello@coachwithkia.com.